Union Public Library

Roundup at the Palace

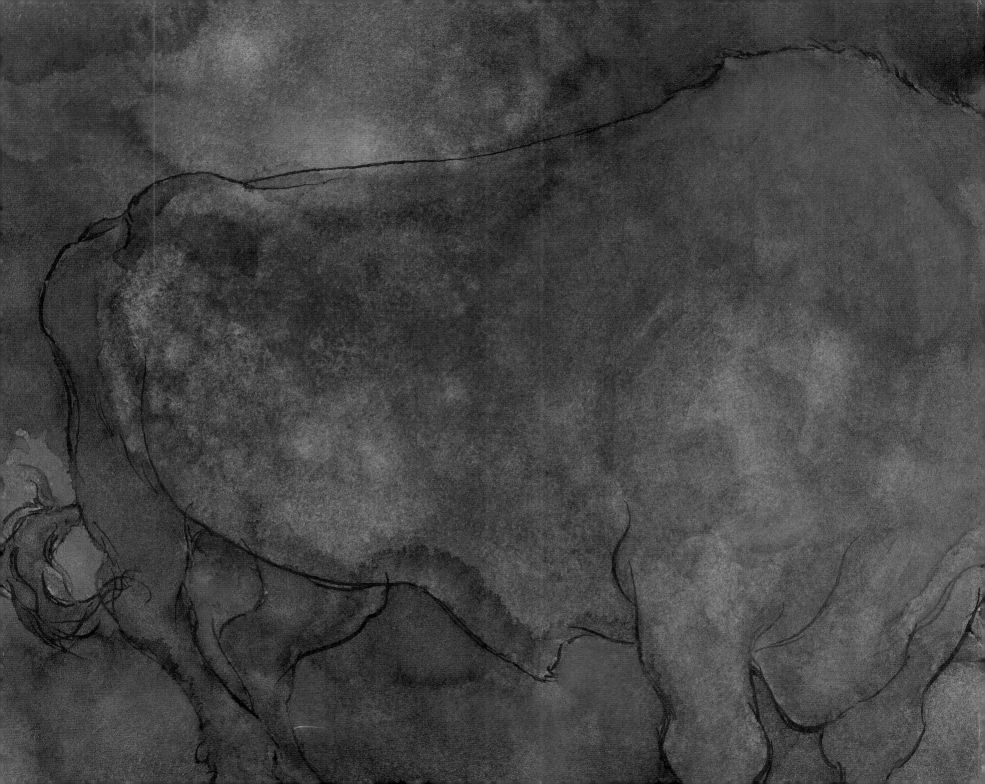

Roundup at the Palace

KATHLEEN COOK WALDRON • ILLUSTRATED BY ALAN & LEA DANIEL

Union Public Library

Red Deer Press

Zack led Buster through the wide barn doors.

Buster sniffed the swirling snow and snorted.
At the ramp leading to the pickup, he stopped
and lowered his head. Zack wrapped his arms
around the huge bull's neck. Buster nuzzled him
gently. "We'll be fine, big guy. You'll see."

Zack hoped this was true. He had never been
to the National Western Stock Show. He'd never
even been to the city. And Buster had never left
the ranch.

When Buster was safely aboard, Zack slapped
the side of the truck. "See you at the Stock Show,"
he said. Then he climbed into the cab with his dad.

The truck bumped down the long driveway,
over rocks and through potholes, to the main road
and the highway.

Zack could feel Buster fidgeting in the back.

"*We'll be comin' round the mountain when we
come,*" Zack and his dad sang as they rode along.
The sky lightened to a pale purple thick with
snowflakes. Trees and mountains slipped by.

"*Come-a-ti-yi-yippee-yippee-yay,*" they sang
through the canyon.

After they'd sung every song they knew, they turned on the radio and sang along with the country tunes.

Zack squinted through the windshield. More and more cars crowded the highway. The snow thickened into a blinding blizzard. Slowly, slowly they crept through the storm. In the back, Buster shuffled and kicked, rocking the truck back and forth. Back and forth.

Inside the pickup cab, the radio announcer said, "Roads are icy, and traffic is backing up. Expect long delays on all highways into Denver."

"Looks like we'll have to detour through downtown," Zack's dad said.

In Denver Alice and her mother stepped outside their tiny downtown apartment into the blowing snow. Through skittering snowflakes, Alice could barely see the banner flapping in the wind:

WELCOME ONE AND ALL
TO THE NATIONAL WESTERN STOCK SHOW,
RODEO, AND HORSE SHOW

"The cowboys are coming today, today," Alice sang softly. "The cowboys are coming. Big yippee-yi-yay."

When the Stock Show came to town, it meant lots of cowboy hats and fancy boots, with tons of horses, cows, and bulls. But Alice had never seen these horses, cows, or bulls. Her downtown apartment didn't even allow cats.

Honking horns and wailing sirens sliced through the wintry air. Snow was piling up on the streets and sidewalks. While waiting for a traffic light, Alice noticed a muddy blue truck creeping along the street.

The truck rocked back and forth—back and forth—to a medley of muffled kicks, grunts, and snorts. Alice tried to peek inside, but her mother hurried her away.

At the wide doors of the Brown Palace Hotel, they said hello to the doorman and stepped inside.

Eight stories above them, a skylight as big as a dance floor lit up the lobby. A lady played a Chopin waltz on the baby grand. Elegant guests glided by or gathered at polished tables to sit and sip tea from fine china cups.

Alice followed her mother across the red carpet, through the lobby, to the hotel gift shop. Here she helped her mother sell toothpaste to movie stars and magazines to businessmen.

Alice-at-the-Palace they called her.

Outside, traffic ground to a halt. Through the snow, Zack stared up at the towering concrete and glass buildings. All he could hear were revving engines, honking horns, howling sirens, and yelling people.

In the back of the pickup Buster fussed. He fidgeted. The truck rocked back and forth. Back and forth. Faster . . . . . . Faster . . . Faster.

All at once, the rocking stopped, and the truck got a whole lot lighter.

"What the . . . ?" Zack and his dad said at the same time. Then they saw Buster. Running down the sidewalk!

Zack grabbed his rope and jumped out
of the truck.

"I can't leave the truck in this traffic,"
Dad yelled. "Stay with Buster, and I'll come
as soon as I can. Don't let him out of your sight!"

As Buster disappeared in the crowd, Zack dashed
past yelling bystanders.

The bull thundered down the sidewalk. Galloping, galloping
toward a set of doors. Wide doors, like the barn doors at home.
   The doors of the Brown Palace Hotel!

Buster roared past the doorman,
nostrils flaring, hooves tearing up the red carpet.

The floor was slippery. Buster skidded.
Guests scattered, screaming. The music stopped.
Alice ran out of the gift shop and into the path of a
steaming, snorting bull!

Buster fixed his eyes on Alice. He lowered his head.

"Don't move," Zack called in a shaky voice. "Talk to him softly, say anything, but say it softly."

Buster pawed the floor. Words spurted out of Alice's mouth.

"Our--our gift shop m--may have just what you're looking for," she stammered. "Candy? Flowers?"

Buster snorted.

Alice swallowed. "Newspaper?"

Buster snorted again.

"Sing to him," Zack called across the lobby. "Singing calms him down."

Buster took a step forward. "Sing what?" Alice asked.

"As I was out walking one cold winter morning," Zack sang.

"As I was out walking one cold winter morning," Alice repeated.

Zack continued, *"I spied a cowpuncher a riding along."*

"I spied a cowpuncher a riding along." Alice joined Zack in a shaky but soothing duet.

Buster flicked his tail. Policemen rushed into the lobby.

Zack's dad was right behind them. He grabbed the first policeman's arm. "Don't move! Don't alarm him. The boy knows what to do."

And sure enough, before an audience eight stories high, Zack eased closer
to Buster and looped his rope through the ring on the bull's halter.

"Now what?" Alice asked.

Zack looked up for the first time and grinned. "Keep singing," he said,
"till Buster's back in the truck."

"Then what?" Alice asked.

"Well," Zack's dad said. "Seems we could use an
extra cowhand. Want to go to the Stock Show?"

"YIP-ee-yi-yay," Alice said, almost forgetting
to say it softly.

Buster swished his tail and left the hotel led
by Zack and Alice. Their voices trailed behind
them, singing, "*Come-a-ti-yi-yippee-*
*yippee-yay, yippee-yay . . . *"

For Alice Toppenberg, the original Alice-at-the-Palace, with special thanks to Norman Granberg for his bullish advice, Alan and Lea Daniel for their talent and enthusiasm, Peter Carver for his perseverance, and everyone at the Brown Palace Hotel, the National Western Stock Show, and the Denver Police Department who graciously answered all my questions and then some.
— Kathleen Cook Waldron

For Peter and Kathy
— Alan and Lea Daniel

Author's note:
The Brown Palace Hotel has been a Denver landmark since 1892. Its guest list has included queens, princes, presidents, film stars, cowboys, miners, horses, bulls, cats, dogs, and even a couple of swarms of bees.

The sixteen-day National Western Stock Show, Rodeo, and Horse Show has been held in Denver every January since 1906, drawing cowboys, ranchers, and other visitors from all over the world. Stormy weather is part of the show's tradition.

Every year, the National Western grand champion steer is exhibited in the Brown Palace lobby during afternoon high tea.

Though Buster is the only bull to have run through the Brown Palace lobby, a champion steer did once escape. In 1996 a gust of wind blew the red carpet into the steer's face as he exited the hotel, causing him to rear up, pull free of his handler, and run the wrong way down a one-way street. Eventually the steer stopped to check out his reflection in a downtown window, allowing his handler to catch up with him.

Copyright © 2006 Kathleen Cook Waldron
Illustration copyright © 2006 Alan & Lea Daniel
Published in the United States in 2006

The right of Kathleen Cook Waldron to be identified as the Author of this Work has been asserted by her.

All rights reserved. No part of this publication may be reproduced, stored in a retrieval system or transmitted, in any form or by any means, without the prior written permission of Red Deer Press or, in case of photocopying or other reprographic copying, a licence from Access Copyright (Canadian Copyright Licensing Agency), 1 Yonge Street, Suite 1900, Toronto, ON M5E 1E5, fax 416-868-1621.

Northern Lights Books for Children are published by Red Deer Press
A Fitzhenry & Whiteside Company, 1512, 1800–4 Street S.W., Calgary, Alberta, Canada T2S 2S5 www.reddeerpress.com

Credits
Edited for the Press by Peter Carver
Design by Blair Kerrigan/Glyphics
Printed and bound in China by Paramount Book Art for Red Deer Press

Acknowledgments
The illustrators thank Kathleen and her family for all their help — and for the great coffee from the Brown Palace Hotel.

Financial support provided by the Canada Council, the Government of Canada through the Book Publishing Industry Development Program (BPIDP).

National Library of Canada Cataloguing in Publication
Waldron, Kathleen Cook
Roundup at the palace / Kathleen Cook Waldron ; illustrated by Alan & Lea Daniel.
(Northern lights books for children)
ISBN 0-88995-319-8

1. Bulls—Juvenile fiction. I. Daniel, Alan, 1939– II. Daniel, Lea III. Title. IV. Series.
PS8595.A549R69 2005   jC813'.54   C2005-904193-5

5 4 3 2 1

The original art for this book was done in pen and ink, and painted in gouache.

Canadä

THE CANADA COUNCIL | LE CONSEIL DES ARTS
FOR THE ARTS | DU CANADA
SINCE 1957 | DEPUIS 1957

FREE PUBLIC LIBRARY UNION, NEW JERSEY

3 9549 00379 2760